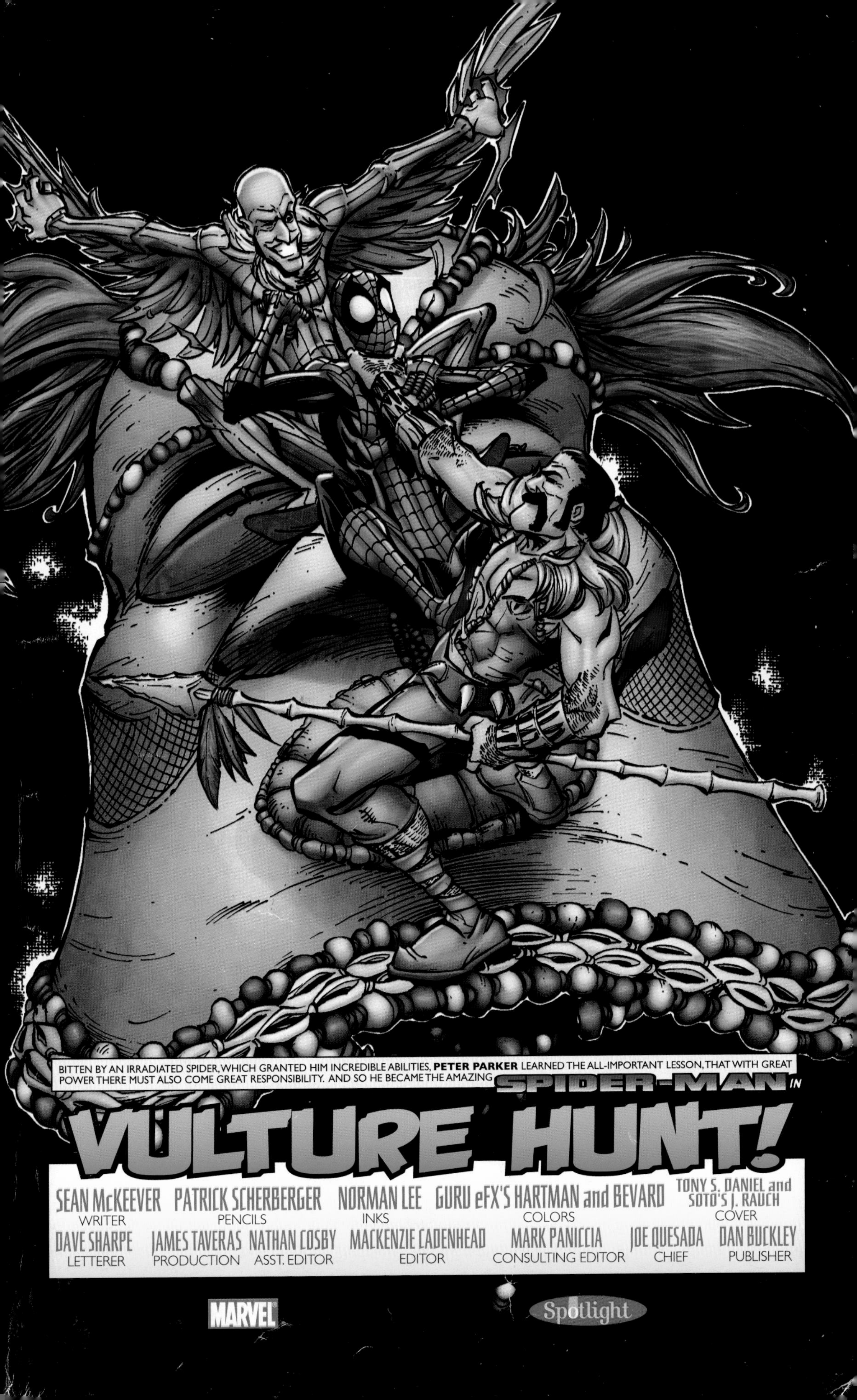

BITTEN BY AN IRRADIATED SPIDER, WHICH GRANTED HIM INCREDIBLE ABILITIES, **PETER PARKER** LEARNED THE ALL-IMPORTANT LESSON, THAT WITH GREAT POWER THERE MUST ALSO COME GREAT RESPONSIBILITY. AND SO HE BECAME THE AMAZING SPIDER-MAN IN

VULTURE HUNT!

SEAN McKEEVER WRITER · PATRICK SCHERBERGER PENCILS · NORMAN LEE INKS · GURU eFX'S HARTMAN and BEVARD COLORS · TONY S. DANIEL and SOTO'S J. RAUCH COVER

DAVE SHARPE LETTERER · JAMES TAVERAS PRODUCTION · NATHAN COSBY ASST. EDITOR · MACKENZIE CADENHEAD EDITOR · MARK PANICCIA CONSULTING EDITOR · JOE QUESADA CHIEF · DAN BUCKLEY PUBLISHER

MARVEL · Spotlight

VISIT US AT
www.abdopublishing.com

Spotlight library bound edition © 2007. Spotlight is a division of ABDO Publishing Company, Edina, Minnesota.

Cataloging Data

McKeever, Sean
    Vulture hunt / Sean McKeever, writer ; Patrick Scherberger, pencils ; Norman Lee, inks. -- Library bound ed.
        p. cm. -- (Spider-Man)
    Summary: Introduces readers of all ages to some of the greatest stories of the legendary Marvel Universe.
    "Marvel age"--Cover.
    Revision of the November 2005 issue of Marvel adventures Spider-Man.
    ISBN-13: 978-1-59961-217-1 (Reinforced Library Bound Edition)
    ISBN-10: 1-59961-217-8 (Reinforced Library Bound Edition)
    1. Spider-Man (Fictitious character)--Fiction. 2. Comic books, strips, etc.-- Fiction. 3. Graphic novels. I. Title. II. Series.

741.5dc22

All Spotlight books are reinforced library binding
and manufactured in the United States of America

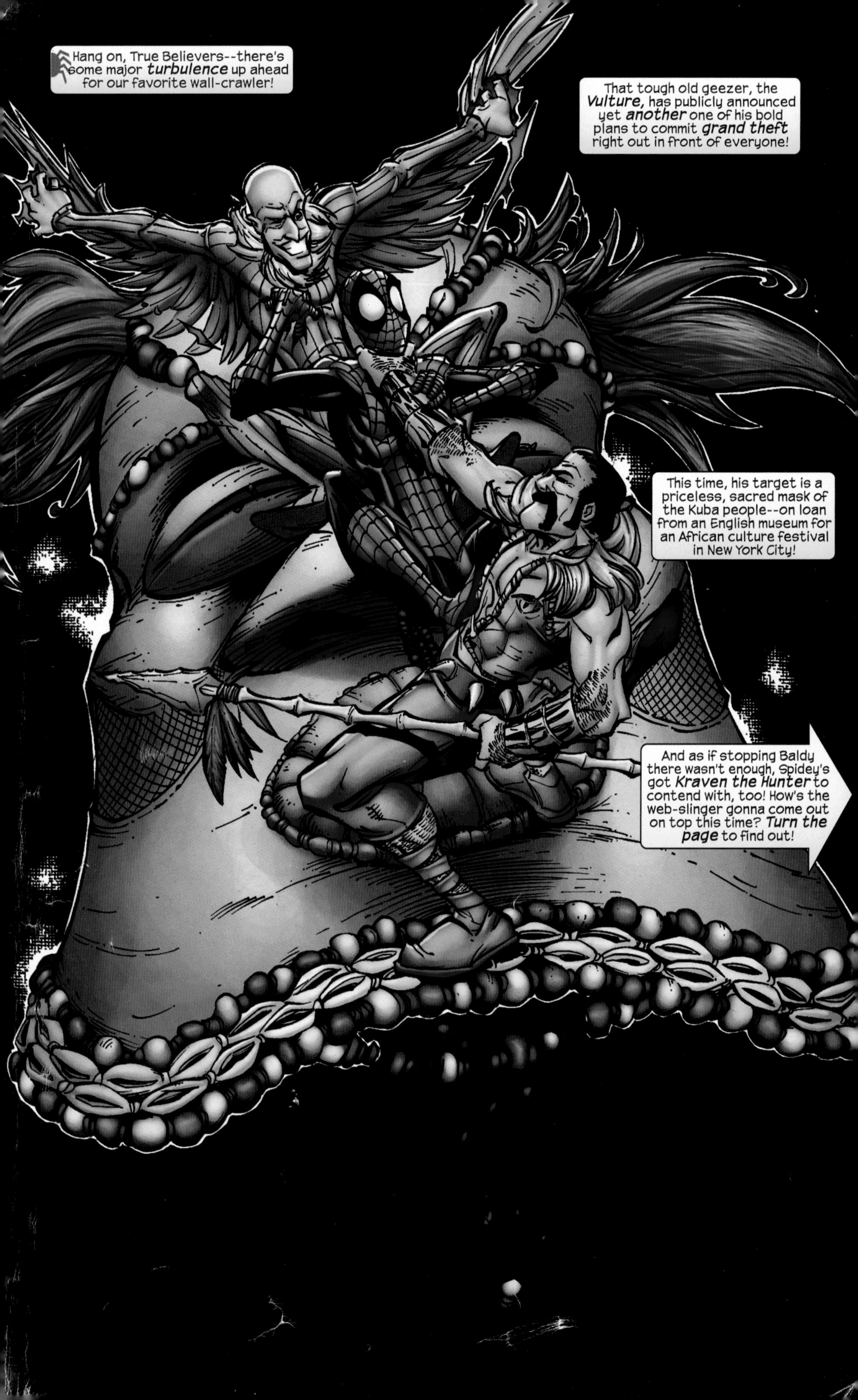
Hang on, True Believers--there's some major turbulence up ahead for our favorite wall-crawler!
That tough old geezer, the Vulture, has publicly announced yet another one of his bold plans to commit grand theft right out in front of everyone!
This time, his target is a priceless, sacred mask of the Kuba people--on loan from an English museum for an African culture festival in New York City!
And as if stopping Baldy there wasn't enough, Spidey's got Kraven the Hunter to contend with, too! How's the web-slinger gonna come out on top this time? Turn the page to find out!

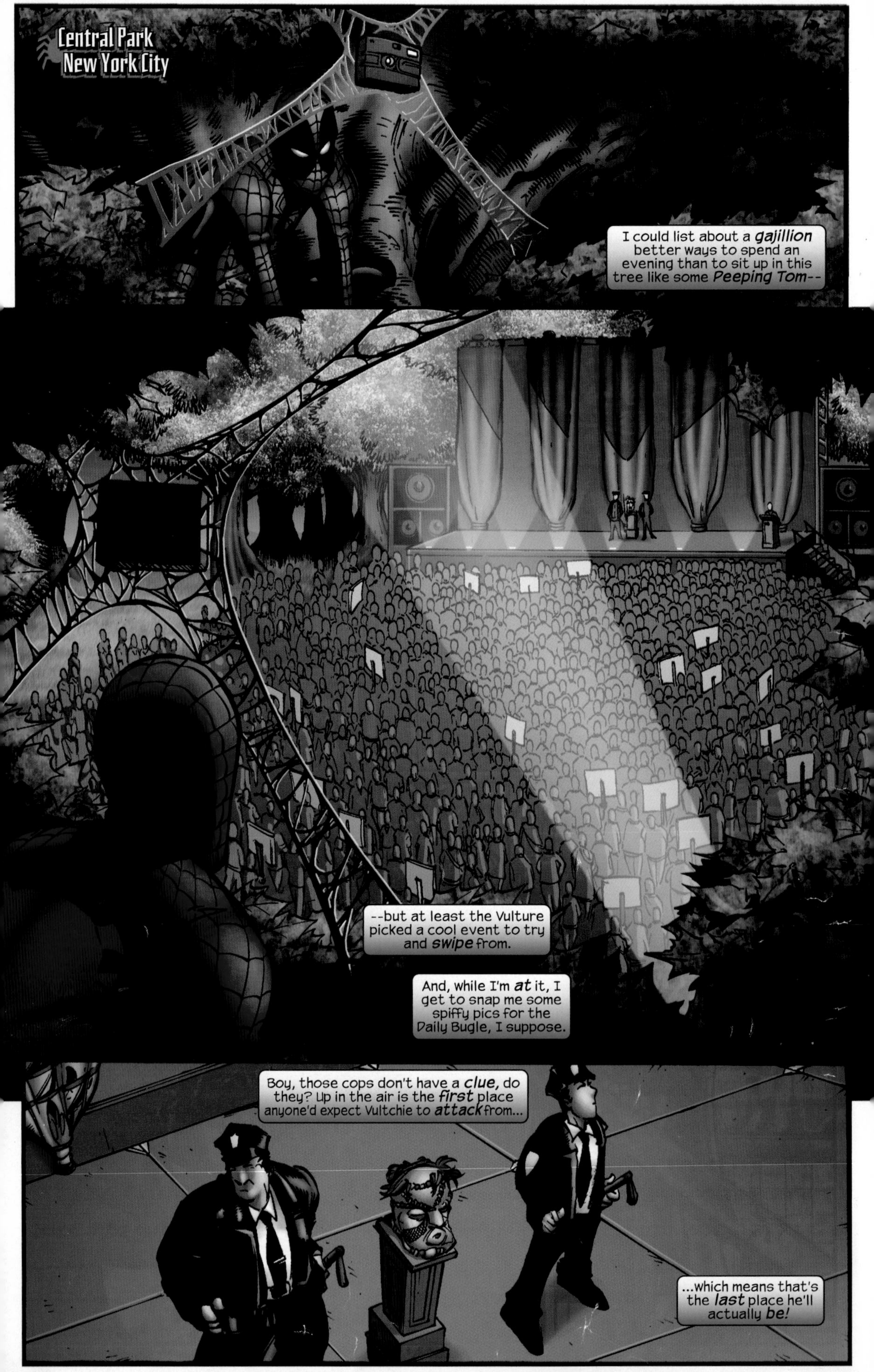
Central Park
New York City
I could list about a *gajillion* better ways to spend an evening than to sit up in this tree like some *Peeping Tom*--
--but at least the Vulture picked a cool event to try and *swipe* from.
And, while I'm *at* it, I get to snap me some spiffy pics for the Daily Bugle, I suppose.
Boy, those cops don't have a *clue*, do they? Up in the air is the *first* place anyone'd expect Vultchie to *attack* from...
...which means that's the *last* place he'll actually *be!*

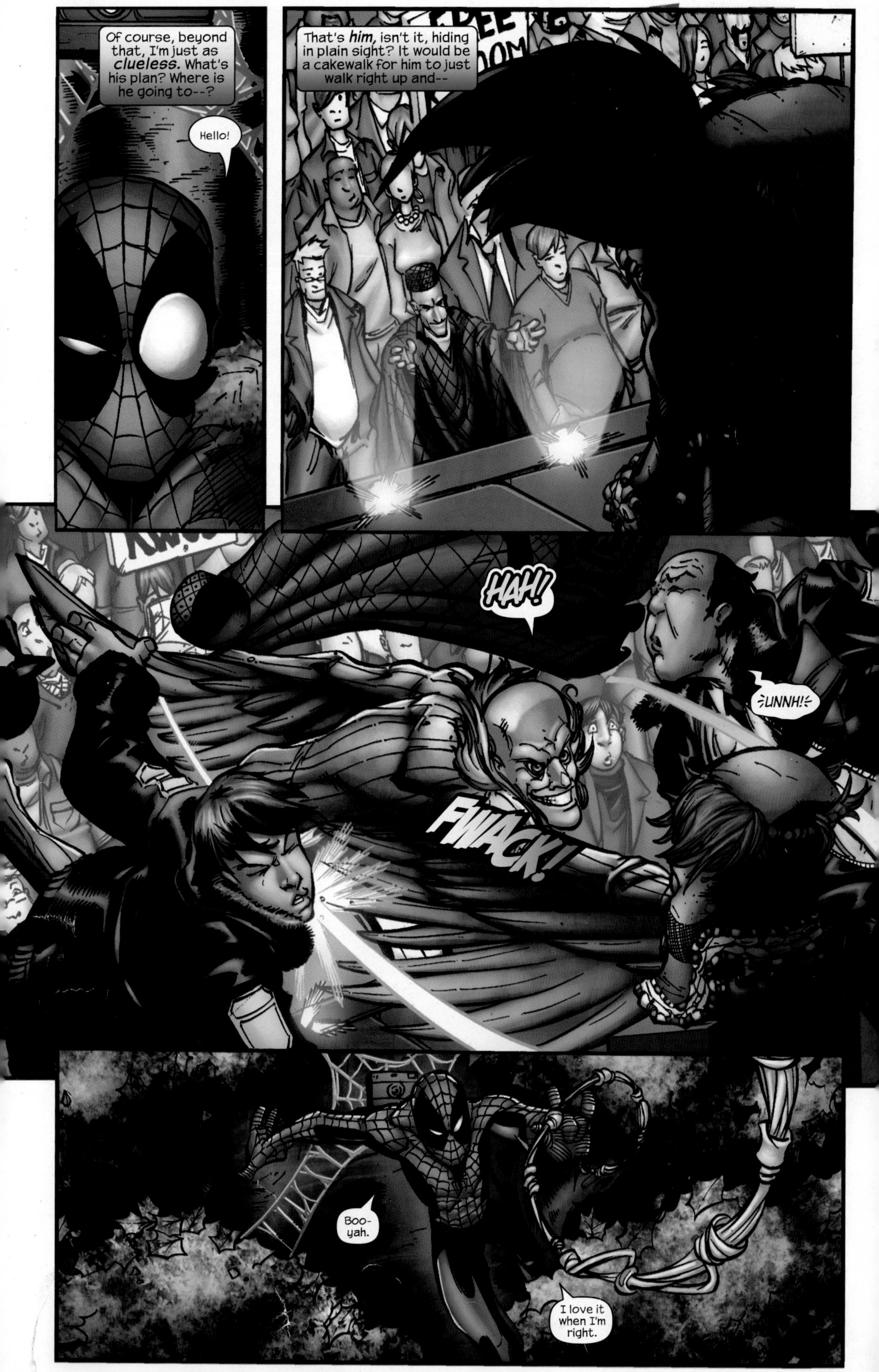

Of course, beyond that, I'm just as *clueless.* What's his plan? Where is he going to--?
Hello!
That's *him,* isn't it, hiding in plain sight? It would be a cakewalk for him to just walk right up and--
HAH!
UNNH!
FWACK!
Boo-yah.
I love it when I'm right.

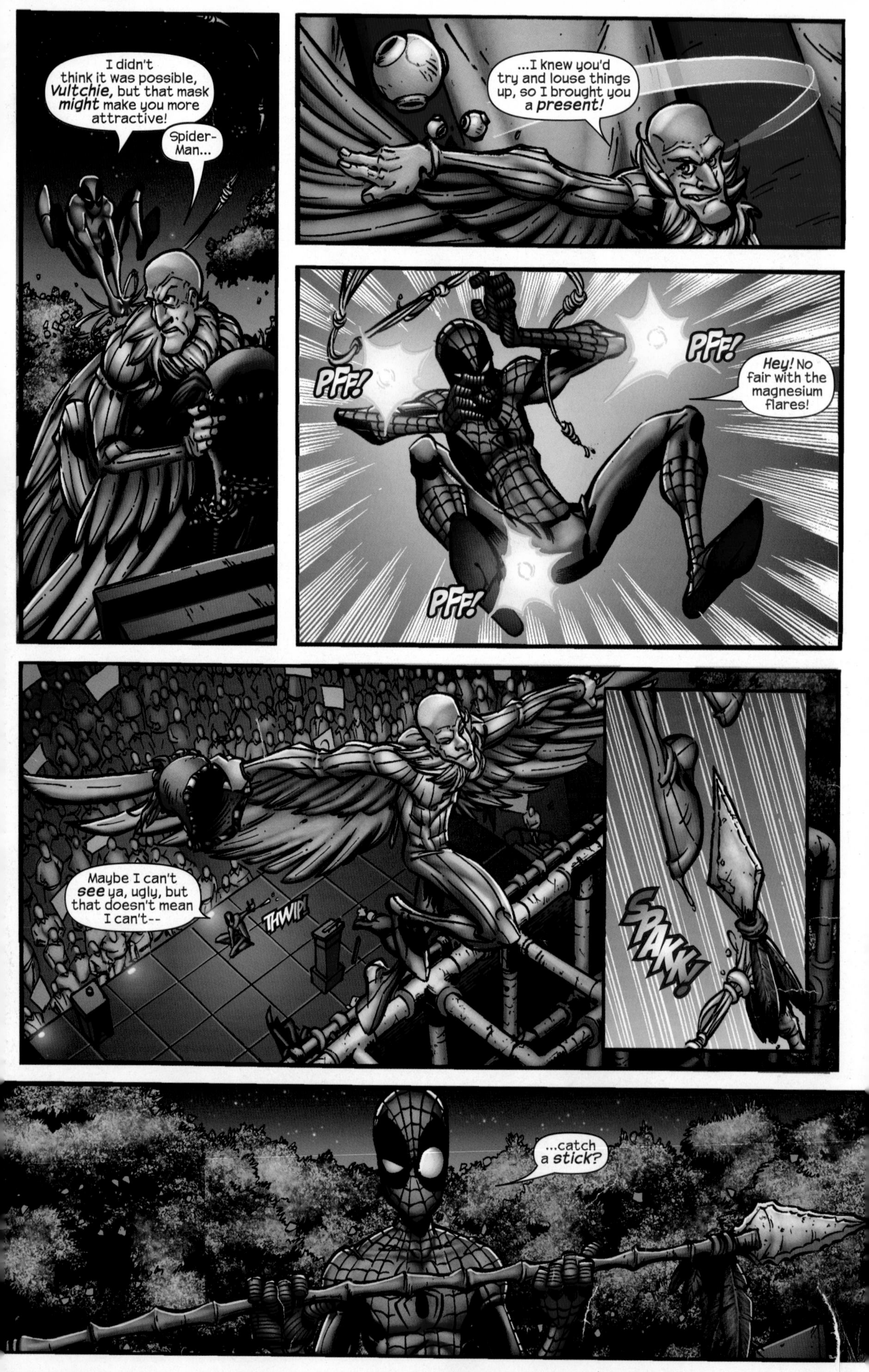
I didn't think it was possible, Vultchie, but that mask might make you more attractive!
Spider-Man...
...I knew you'd try and louse things up, so I brought you a present!
PFF!
PFF!
Hey! No fair with the magnesium flares!
PFF!
Maybe I can't see ya, ugly, but that doesn't mean I can't--
THWIP!
SPAKK!
...catch a stick?

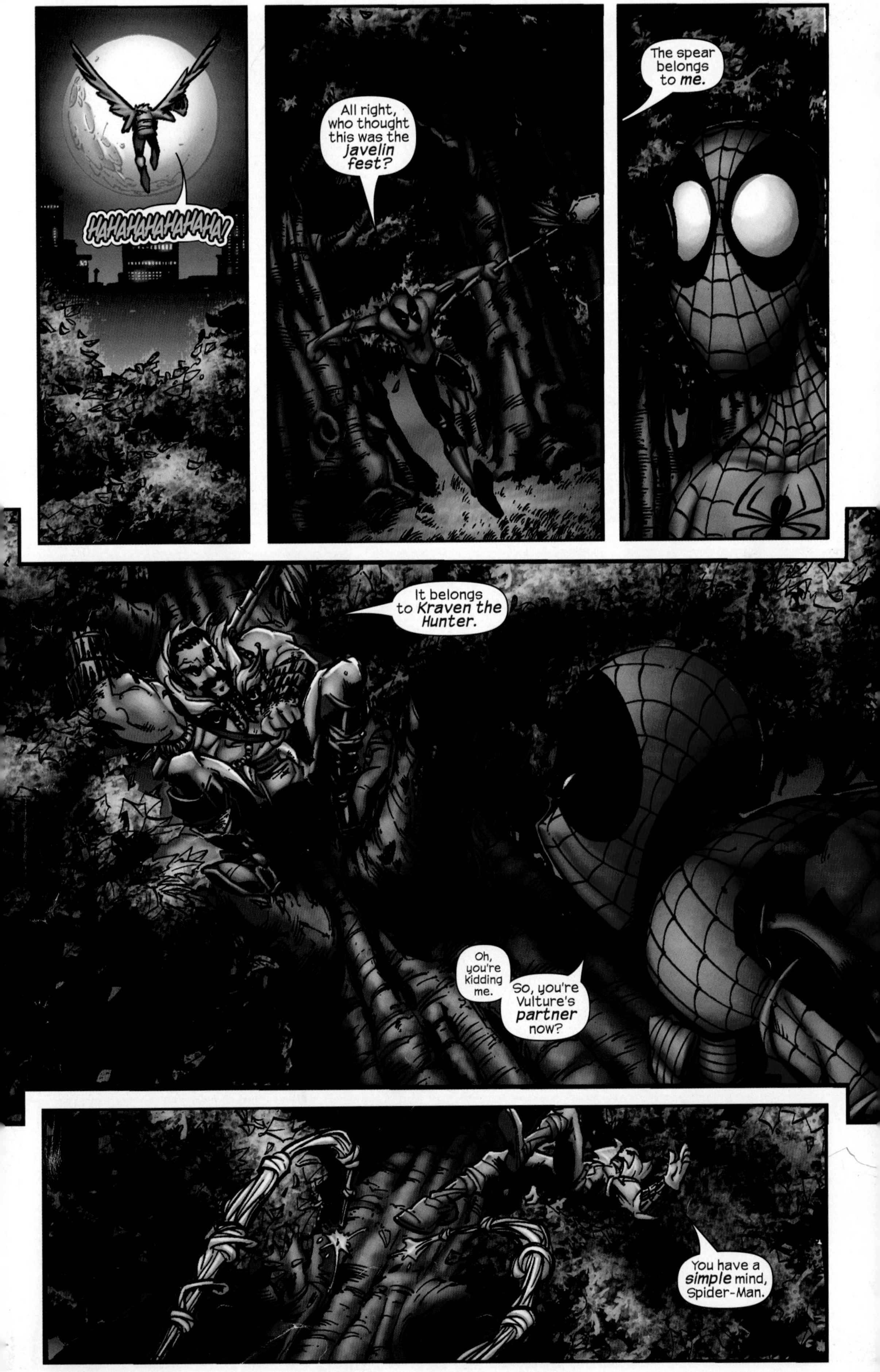
HAHAHAHAHAHAHA!
All right, who thought this was the *javelin fest?*
The spear belongs to ***me.***
It belongs to *Kraven the Hunter.*
Oh, you're kidding me.
So, you're Vulture's ***partner*** now?
You have a ***simple*** mind, Spider-Man.

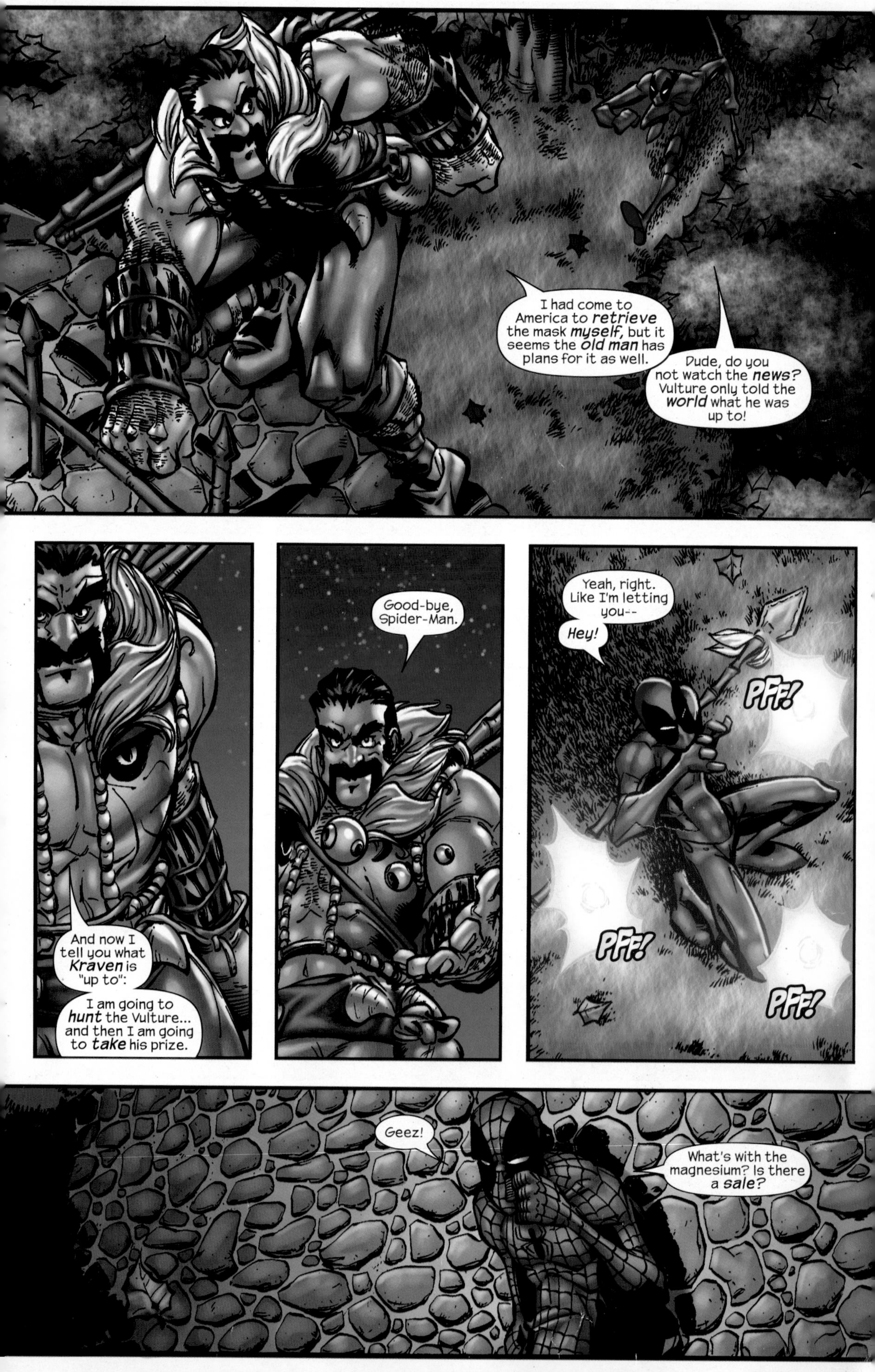
I had come to America to retrieve the mask myself, but it seems the old man has plans for it as well.
Dude, do you not watch the news? Vulture only told the world what he was up to!
And now I tell you what Kraven is "up to":
I am going to hunt the Vulture... and then I am going to take his prize.
Good-bye, Spider-Man.
Yeah, right. Like I'm letting you--
Hey!
PFF!
PFF!
PFF!
Geez!
What's with the magnesium? Is there a sale?

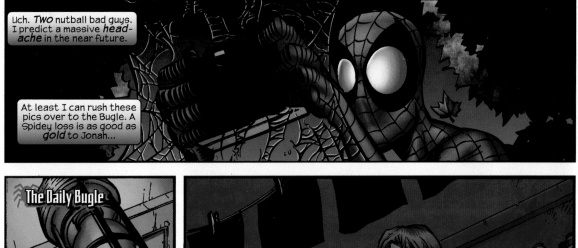

Uch. *TWO* nutball bad guys. I predict a massive *head-ache* in the near future.

At least I can rush these pics over to the Bugle. A Spidey loss is as good as *gold* to Jonah...

The Daily Bugle

DARK ROOM

Aw, man...!

Is this some kinda *joke?*

These've gotta be the *worst,* most *unprofessional* shots I've ever seen--

--and I've seen 'em *all!*

If you wanna get an *art* degree, Parker, you can do it on your *own* dime! I buy shots that sell papers--*period!*

Speaking of which...

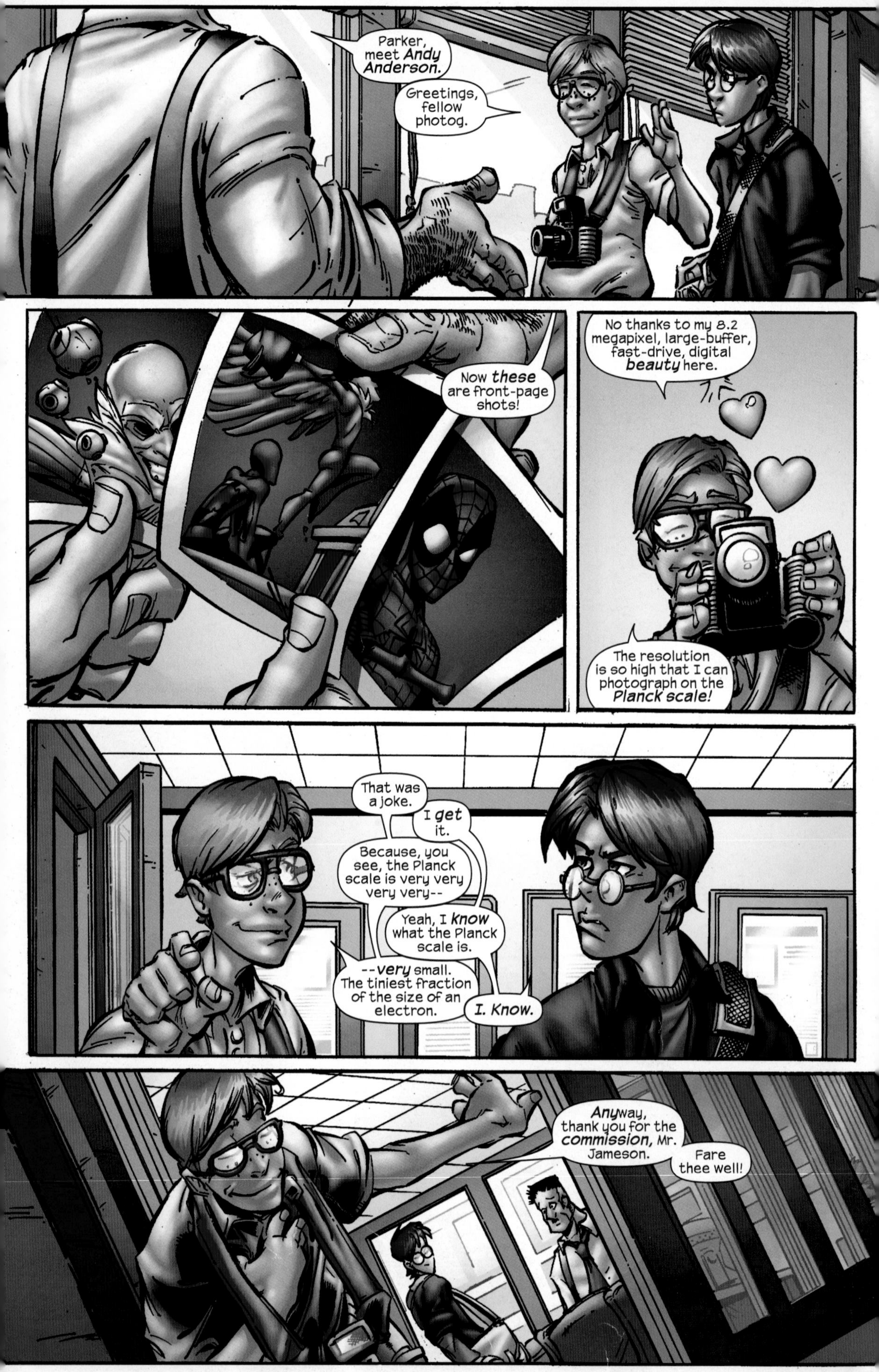

Parker, meet *Andy Anderson.*
Greetings, fellow photog.
Now *these* are front-page shots!
No thanks to my 8.2 megapixel, large-buffer, fast-drive, digital *beauty* here.
The resolution is so high that I can photograph on the *Planck scale!*
That was a joke.
I *get* it.
Because, you see, the Planck scale is very very very very--
Yeah, I *know* what the Planck scale is.
--*very* small. The tiniest fraction of the size of an electron.
I. Know.
*Any*way, thank you for the *commission,* Mr. Jameson.
Fare thee well!

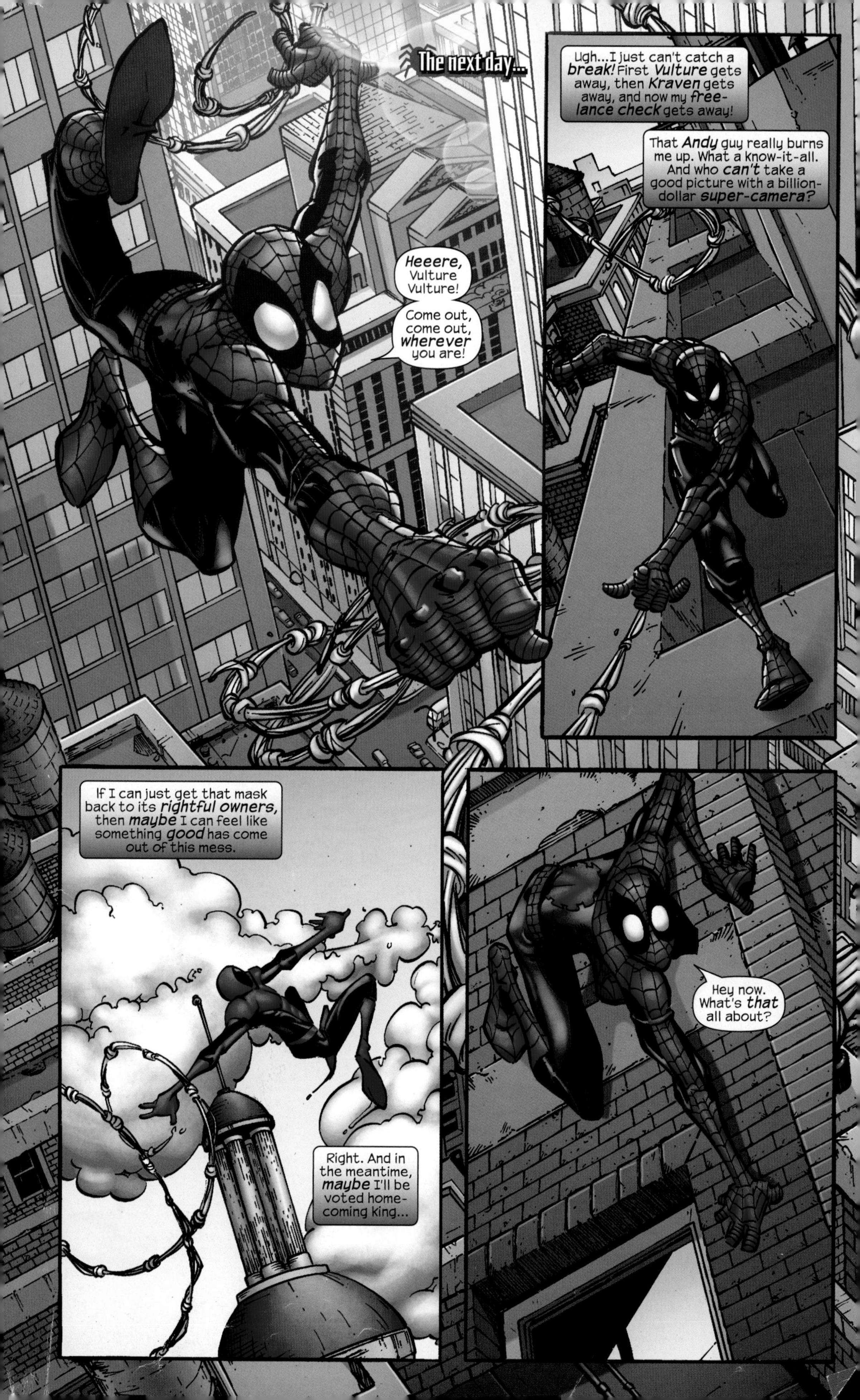
The next day...
Heeere, Vulture Vulture!
Come out, come out, wherever you are!
Ugh...I just can't catch a break! First Vulture gets away, then Kraven gets away, and now my free-lance check gets away!
That Andy guy really burns me up. What a know-it-all. And who can't take a good picture with a billion-dollar super-camera?
If I can just get that mask back to its rightful owners, then maybe I can feel like something good has come out of this mess.
Right. And in the meantime, maybe I'll be voted home-coming king...
Hey now. What's that all about?

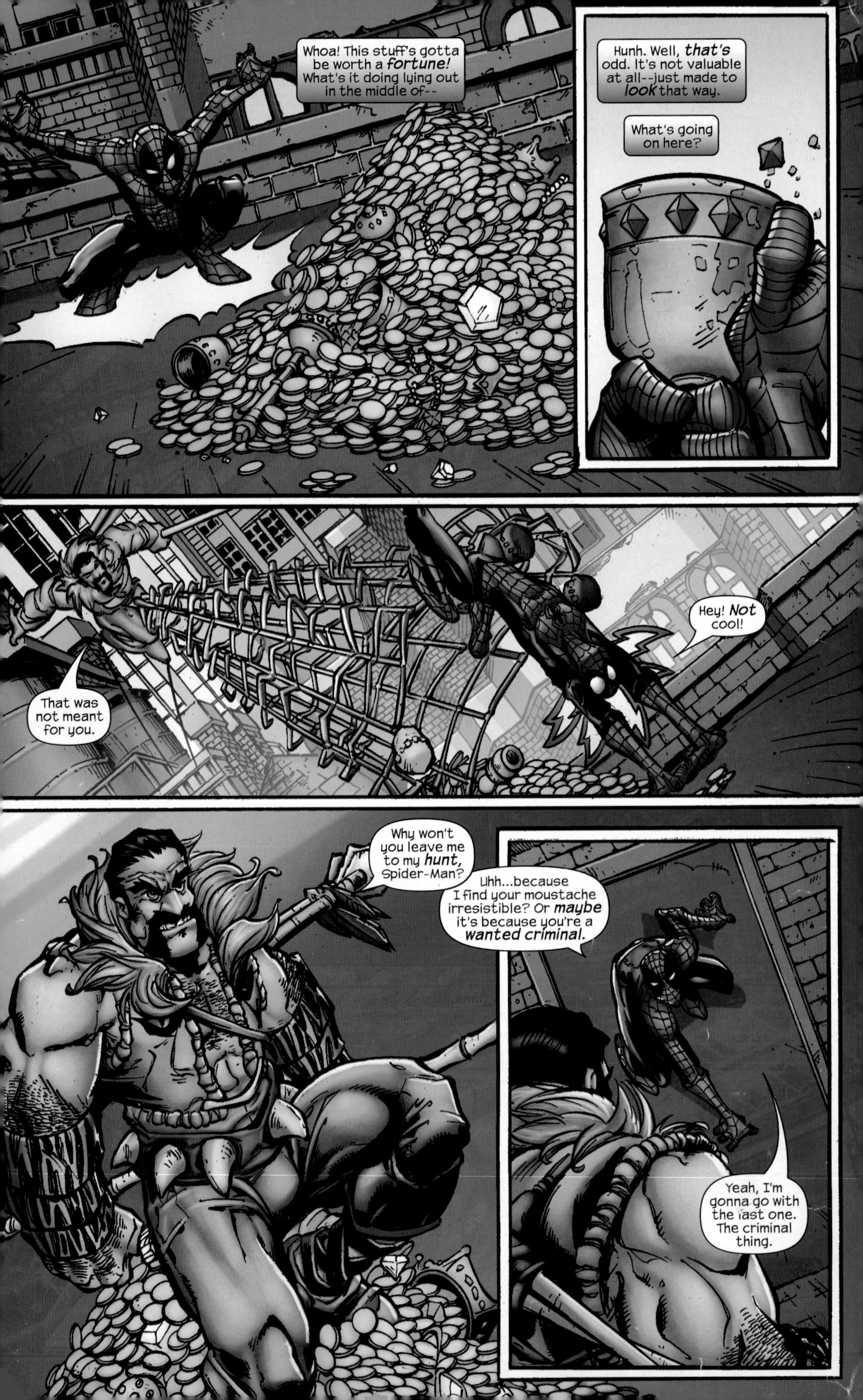

Whoa! This stuff's gotta be worth a *fortune!* What's it doing lying out in the middle of--
Hunh. Well, ***that's*** odd. It's not valuable at all--just made to ***look*** that way.
What's going on here?
Hey! ***Not*** cool!
That was not meant for you.
Why won't you leave me to my ***hunt,*** Spider-Man?
Uhh...because I find your moustache irresistible? Or ***maybe*** it's because you're a ***wanted criminal.***
Yeah, I'm gonna go with the last one. The criminal thing.

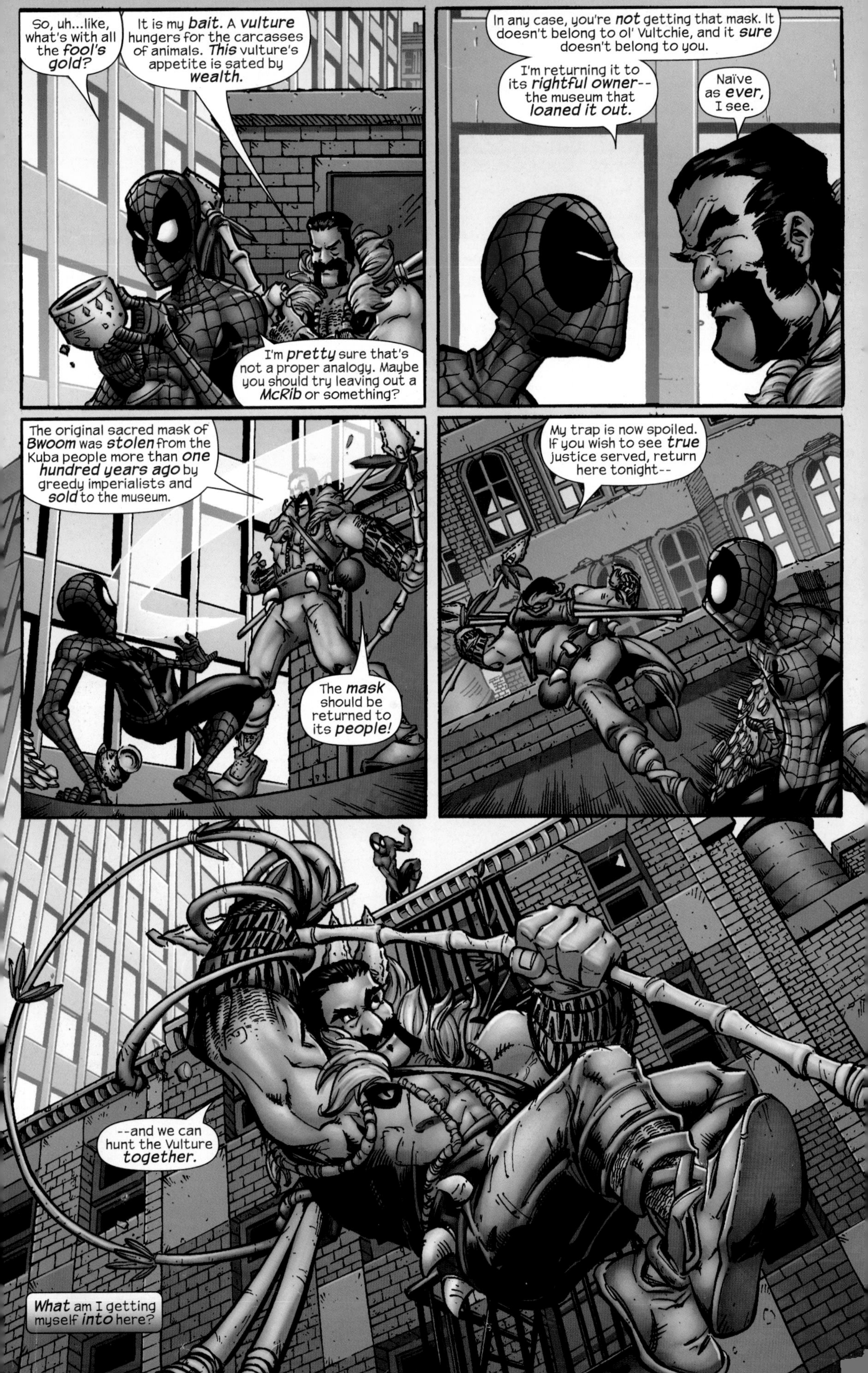
So, uh...like, what's with all the fool's gold?
It is my bait. A vulture hungers for the carcasses of animals. This vulture's appetite is sated by wealth.
I'm pretty sure that's not a proper analogy. Maybe you should try leaving out a McRib or something?
In any case, you're not getting that mask. It doesn't belong to ol' Vultchie, and it sure doesn't belong to you.
I'm returning it to its rightful owner--the museum that loaned it out.
Naïve as ever, I see.
The original sacred mask of Bwoom was stolen from the Kuba people more than one hundred years ago by greedy imperialists and sold to the museum.
The mask should be returned to its people!
My trap is now spoiled. If you wish to see true justice served, return here tonight--
--and we can hunt the Vulture together.
What am I getting myself into here?

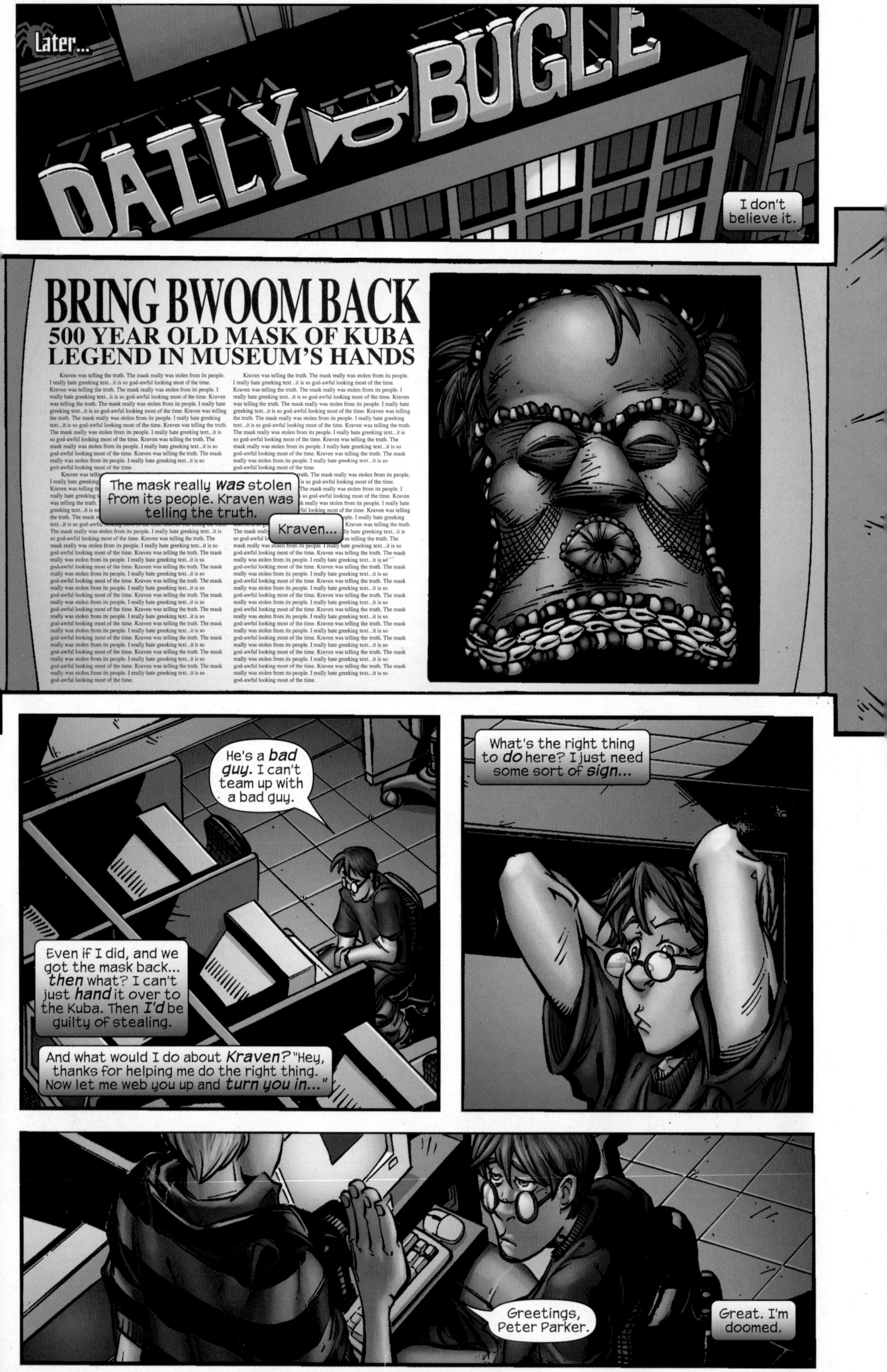
Later...
DAILY BUGLE
I don't believe it.
BRING BWOOM BACK
500 YEAR OLD MASK OF KUBA LEGEND IN MUSEUM'S HANDS
The mask really *was* stolen from its people. Kraven was telling the truth.
Kraven...
He's a *bad guy.* I can't team up with a bad guy.
Even if I did, and we got the mask back... *then* what? I can't just *hand* it over to the Kuba. Then *I'd* be guilty of stealing.
And what would I do about *Kraven?* "Hey, thanks for helping me do the right thing. Now let me web you up and *turn you in...*"
What's the right thing to *do* here? I just need some sort of *sign...*
Greetings, Peter Parker.
Great. I'm doomed.

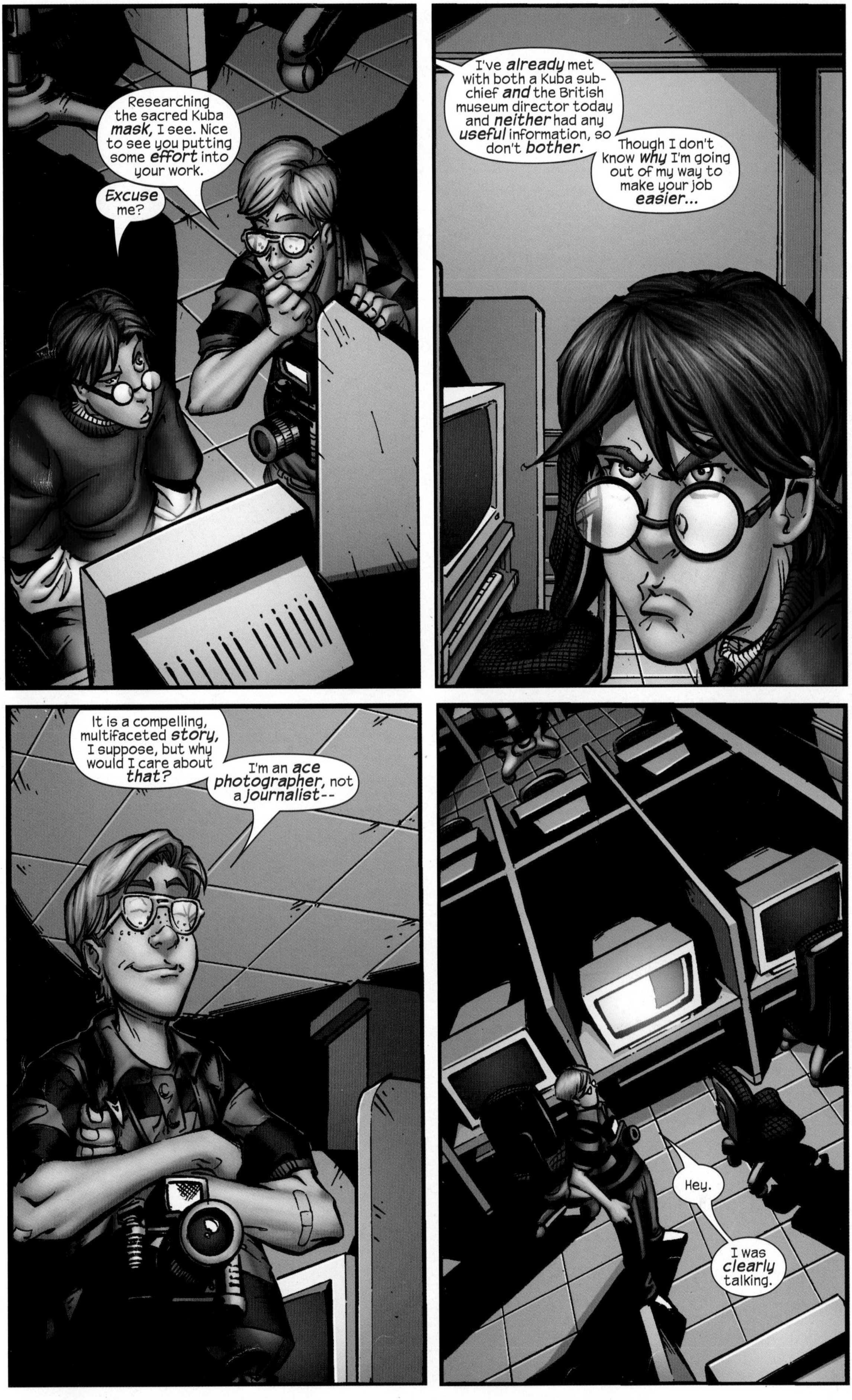
Researching the sacred Kuba mask, I see. Nice to see you putting some effort into your work.
Excuse me?
I've already met with both a Kuba sub-chief and the British museum director today and neither had any useful information, so don't bother.
Though I don't know why I'm going out of my way to make your job easier...
It is a compelling, multifaceted story, I suppose, but why would I care about that?
I'm an ace photographer, not a journalist--
Hey.
I was clearly talking.

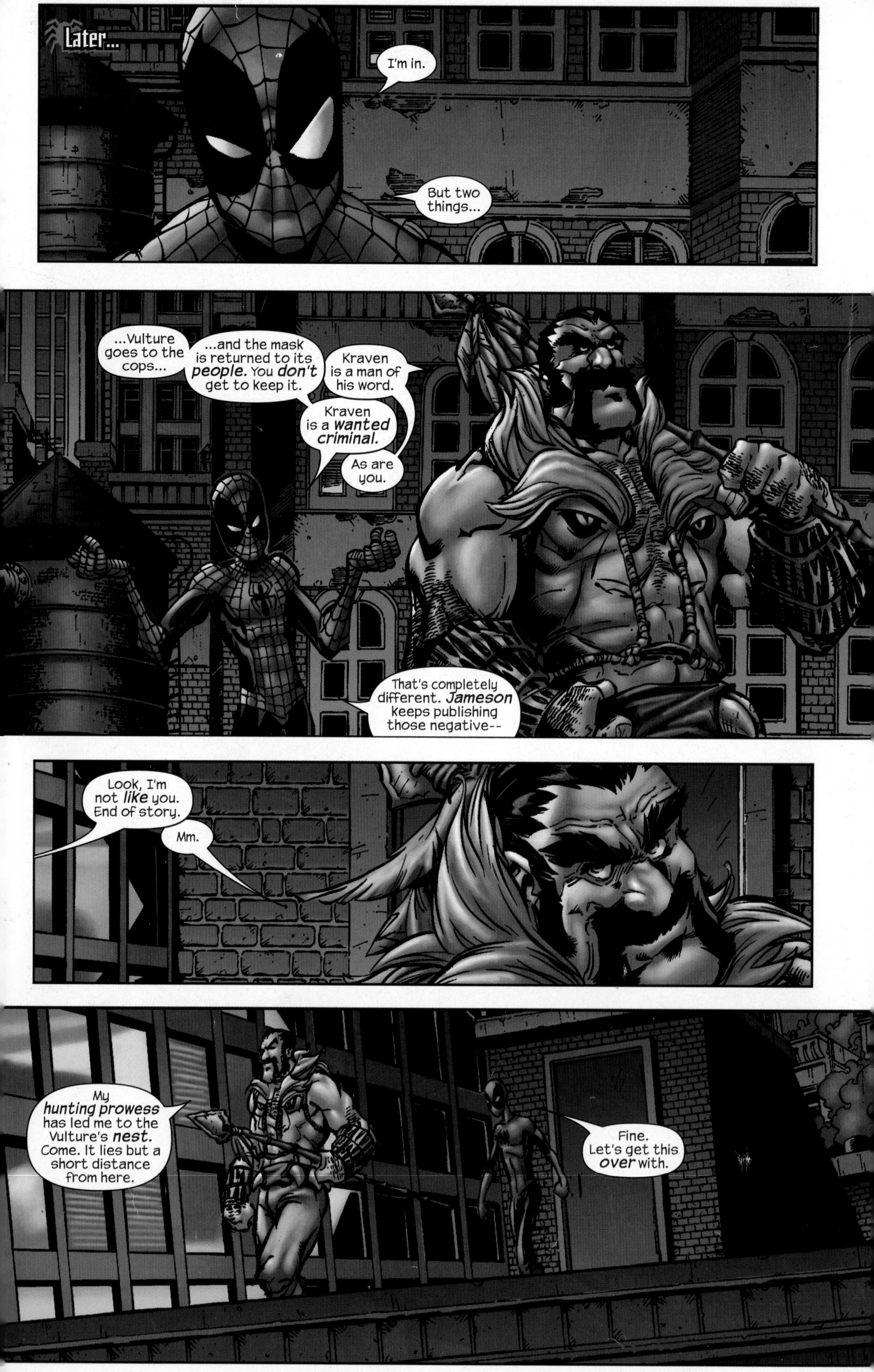
Later...
I'm in.
But two things...
...Vulture goes to the cops...
...and the mask is returned to its people. You don't get to keep it.
Kraven is a man of his word.
Kraven is a wanted criminal.
As are you.
That's completely different. Jameson keeps publishing those negative--
Look, I'm not like you. End of story.
Mm.
My hunting prowess has led me to the Vulture's nest. Come. It lies but a short distance from here.
Fine. Let's get this over with.

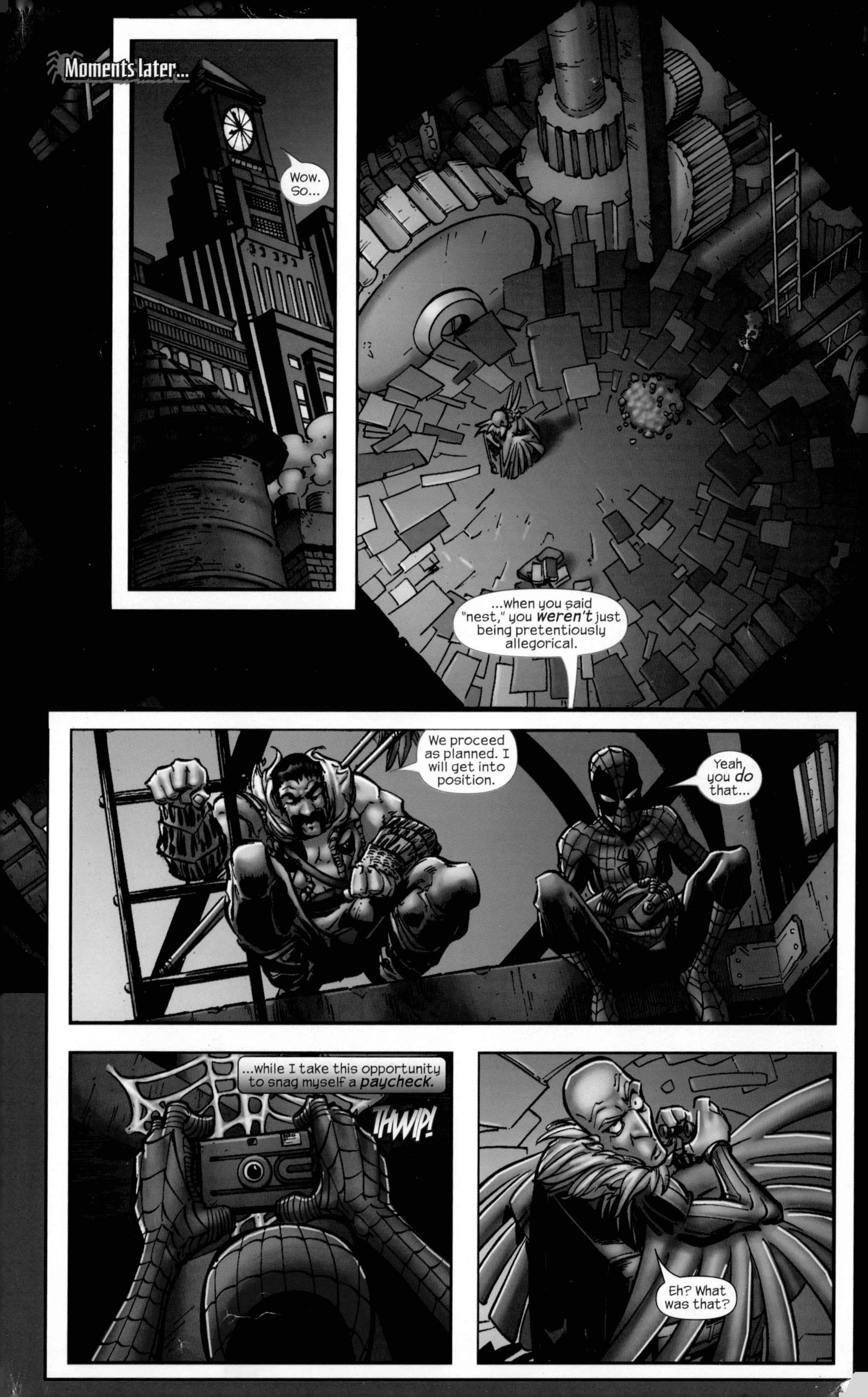
Moments later...
Wow. So...
...when you said "nest," you weren't just being pretentiously allegorical.
We proceed as planned. I will get into position.
Yeah, you do that...
...while I take this opportunity to snag myself a paycheck.
THWIP!
Eh? What was that?

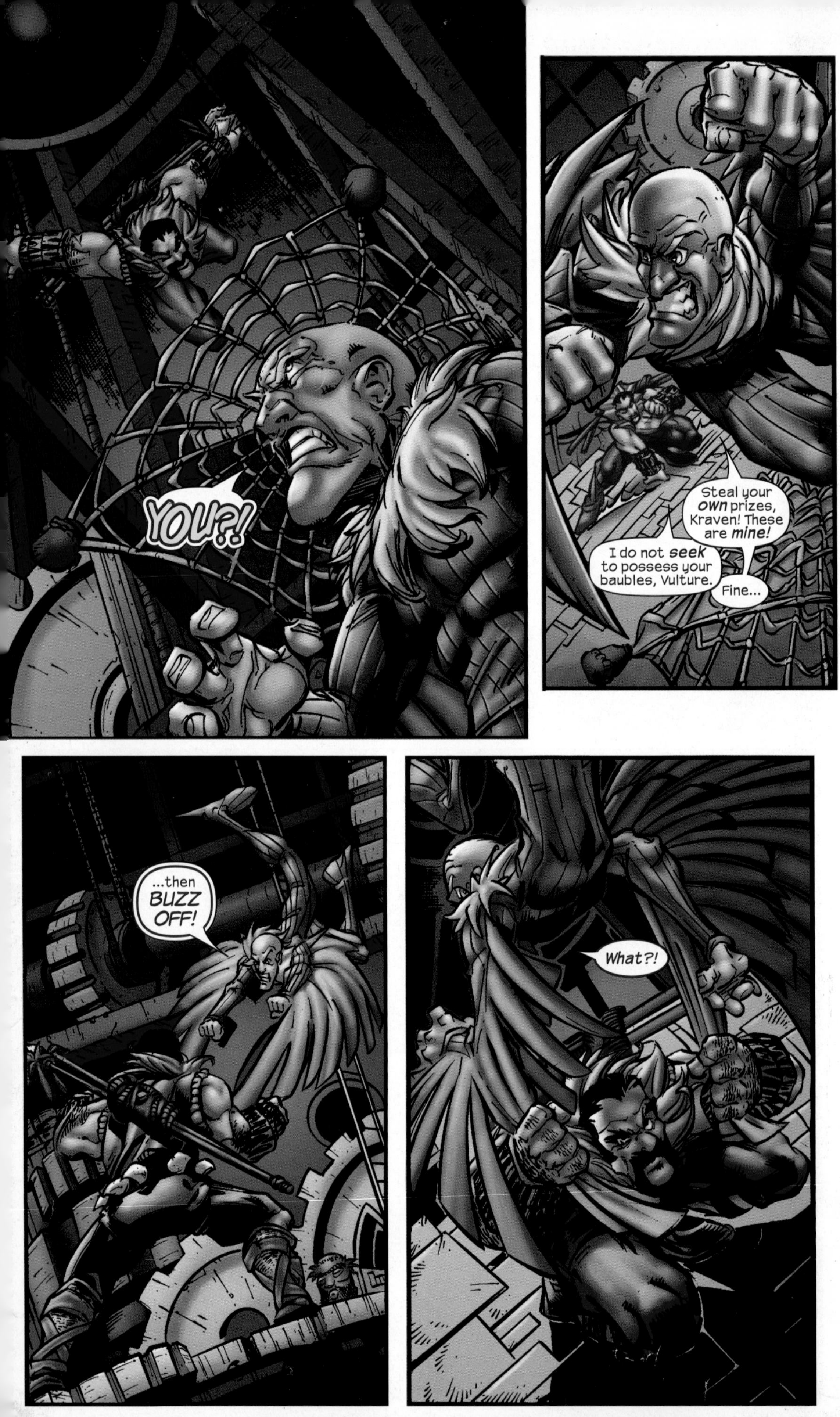
YOU?!
Steal your OWN prizes, Kraven! These are mine!
I do not seek to possess your baubles, Vulture.
Fine...
...then BUZZ OFF!
What?!

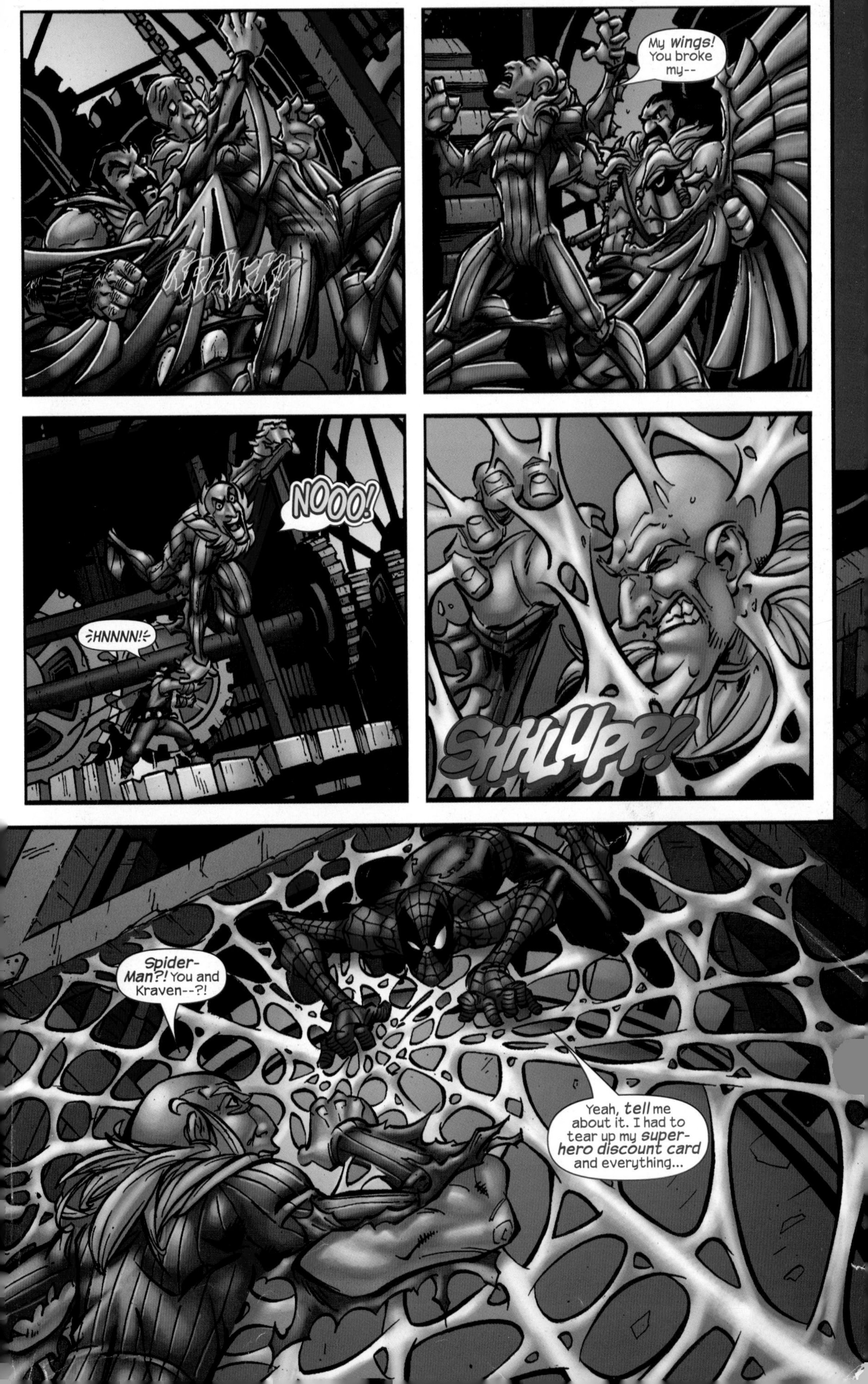
KRAKK!
My wings! You broke my--
NOOO!
HNNNN!
SHHLUPP!
Spider-Man?! You and Kraven--?!
Yeah, tell me about it. I had to tear up my super-hero discount card and everything...

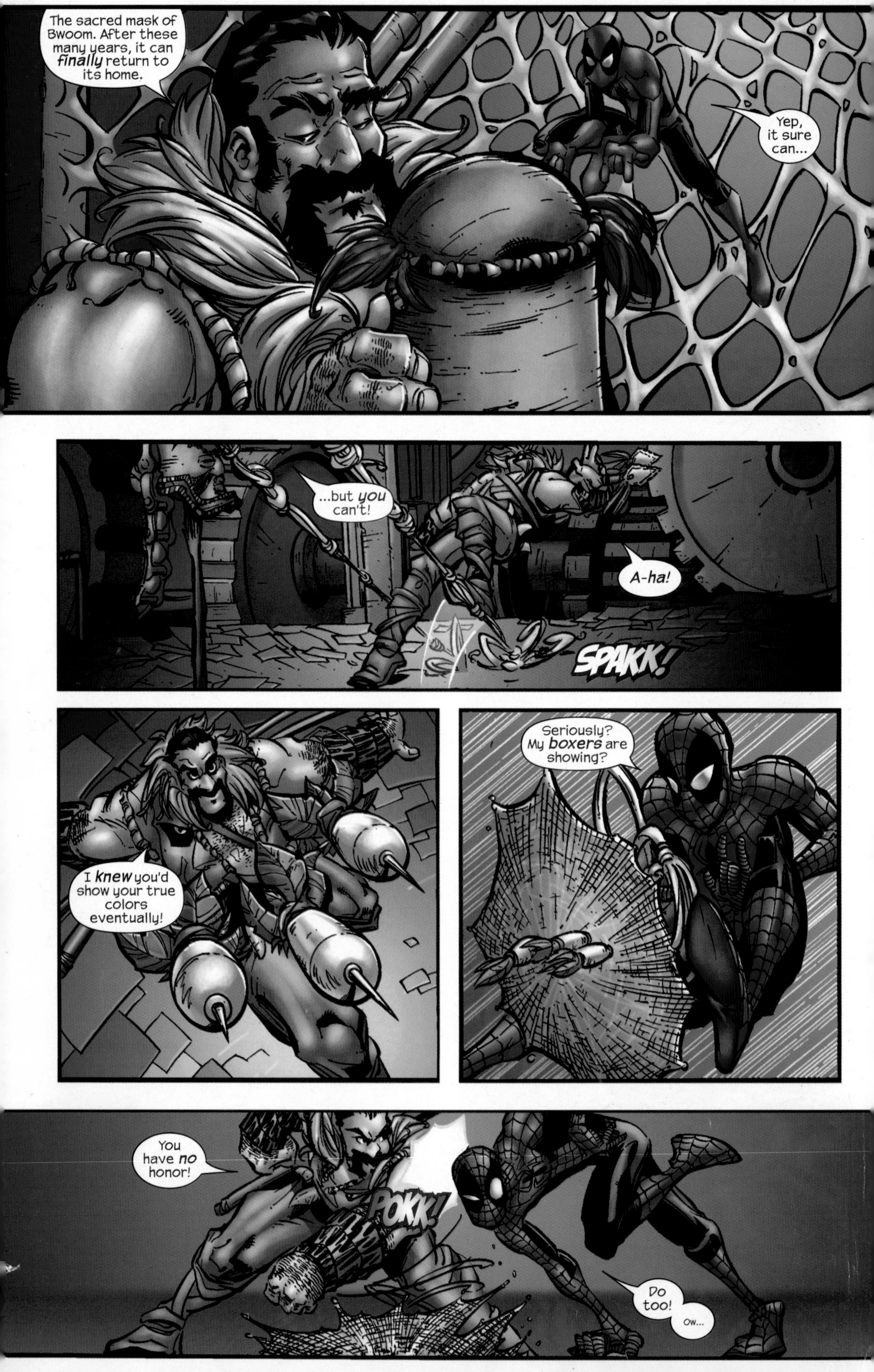
The sacred mask of Bwoom. After these many years, it can *finally* return to its home.
Yep, it sure can...
...but *you* can't!
A-ha!
SPAKK!
I *knew* you'd show your true colors eventually!
Seriously? My *boxers* are showing?
You have *no* honor!
POKK!
Do too!
ow...

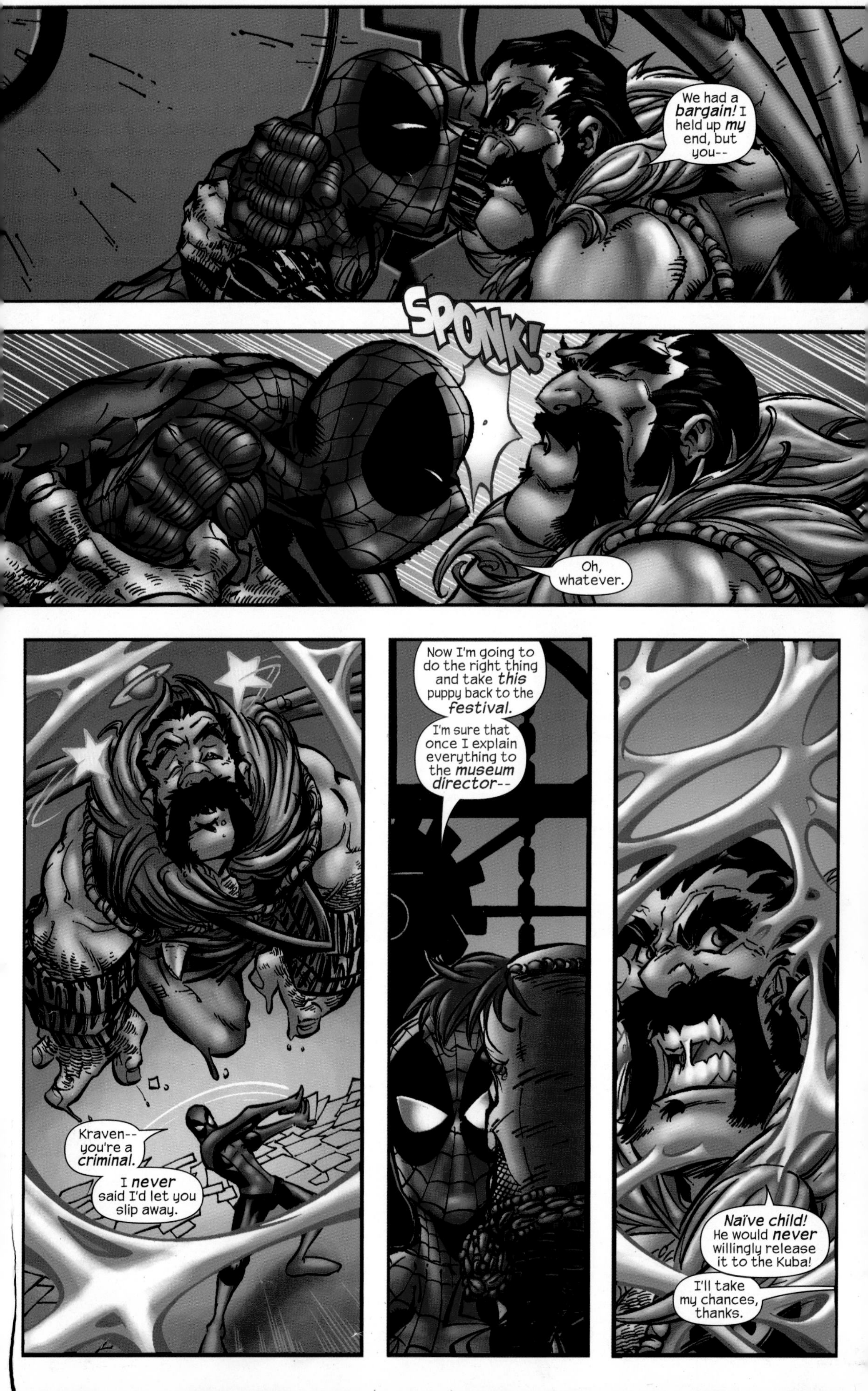
We had a bargain! I held up my end, but you--
SPONK!
Oh, whatever.
Kraven-- you're a criminal.
I never said I'd let you slip away.
Now I'm going to do the right thing and take this puppy back to the festival.
I'm sure that once I explain everything to the museum director--
Naïve child! He would never willingly release it to the Kuba!
I'll take my chances, thanks.

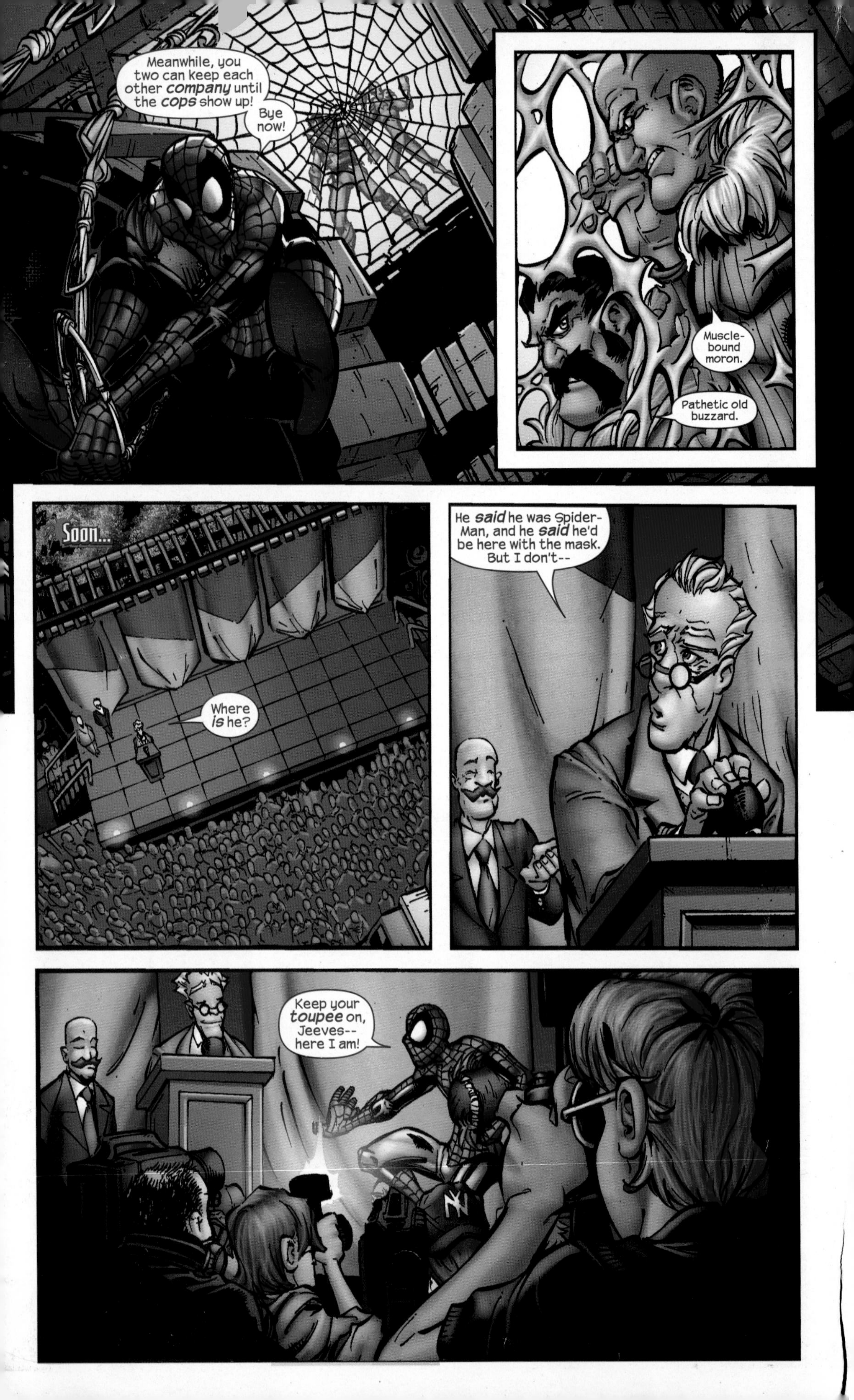

Meanwhile, you two can keep each other *company* until the *cops* show up!
Bye now!
Muscle-bound moron.
Pathetic old buzzard.
Soon...
Where *is* he?
He *said* he was Spider-Man, and he *said* he'd be here with the mask. But I don't--
Keep your *toupee* on, Jeeves-- here I am!

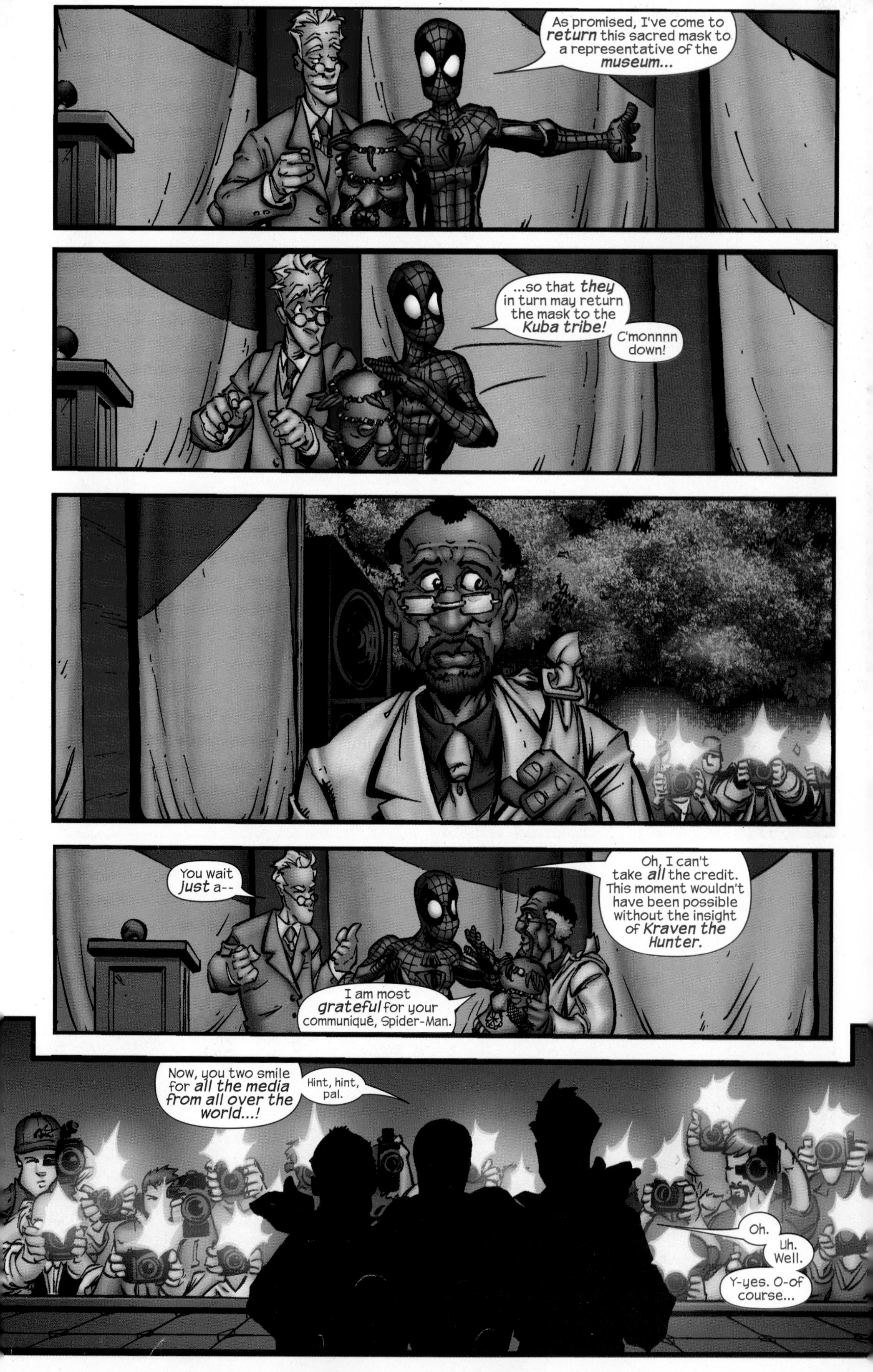
As promised, I've come to return this sacred mask to a representative of the museum...
...so that they in turn may return the mask to the Kuba tribe!
C'monnnn down!
You wait just a--
Oh, I can't take all the credit. This moment wouldn't have been possible without the insight of Kraven the Hunter.
I am most grateful for your communiqué, Spider-Man.
Now, you two smile for all the media from all over the world...!
Hint, hint, pal.
Oh.
Uh. Well.
Y-yes. O-of course...

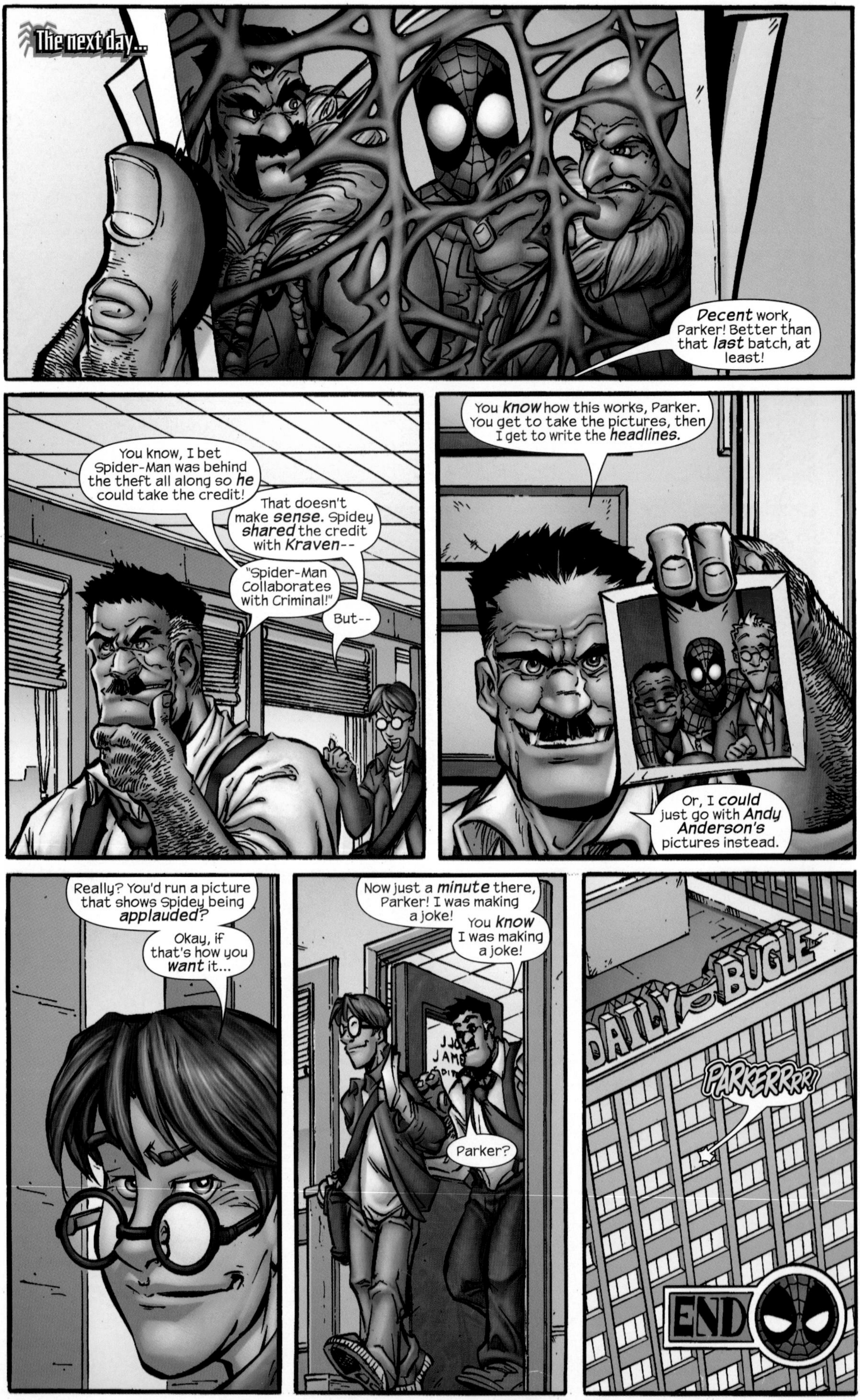
The next day...
Decent work, Parker! Better than that last batch, at least!
You know, I bet Spider-Man was behind the theft all along so he could take the credit!
That doesn't make sense. Spidey shared the credit with Kraven--
"Spider-Man Collaborates with Criminal!"
But--
You know how this works, Parker. You get to take the pictures, then I get to write the headlines.
Or, I could just go with Andy Anderson's pictures instead.
Really? You'd run a picture that shows Spidey being applauded?
Okay, if that's how you want it...
Now just a minute there, Parker! I was making a joke!
You know I was making a joke!
Parker?
DAILY BUGLE
PARKERRRR!
END